Cake & I Scream!

To John, my husband and dearest friend of thirty years—thank you for all of your loving support!—*MG*

For all who love cake. For all who love ice cream. For all who love reading!—*SM*

Published by
MAGINATION PRESS ®
An Educational Publishing Foundation Book
American Psychological Association
750 First Street NE
Washington, DC 20002

Magination Press is a registered trademark of the American Psychological Association.

For more information about our books, including a complete catalog, please write to us, call 1-800-374-2721, or visit our website at www.apa.org/pubs/magination.

Book design by Sandra Kimbell
Printed by Lake Book Manufacturing, Inc., Melrose Park, IL
Cookie Nookie font by Typadelic

Library of Congress Cataloging-in-Publication Data
Names: Genhart, Michael, author. | Mack, Steve
  (Steve Page), illustrator.
Title: Cake & I scream! : ... being bossy isn't sweet /
  by Michael Genhart, PhD ; illustrated by Steve Mack.
Other titles: Cake and I scream!
Description: Washington, DC : Magination Press, an
  imprint of the American Psychological Association,
  [2017] | Summary: Cake tells about his friend,
  Ice Cream, who tries to get his way by being bossy
  and loud, only to find out that is a good way to lose
  friends.
Identifiers: LCCN 2016050560| ISBN 9781433827594
  (hardcover) | ISBN 143382759X (hardcover)
Subjects: | CYAC: Behavior—Fiction. | Friendship—
  Fiction. | Ice cream, ices, etc.—Fiction. | Cake—Fiction.
Classification: LCC PZ7.1.G47 Cak 2017 | DDC
  [E]—dc23 LC record available at
  https://lccn.loc.gov/2016050560

Manufactured in the United States of America
10 9 8 7 6 5 4 3 2 1

Cake & I Scream!

...being bossy isn't sweet

by Michael Genhart, PhD   illustrated by Steve Mack

Magination Press • Washington, DC
American Psychological Association

I'm a pretty basic guy. But don't let that fool you.
There are many layers to my personality.

I am firm, and I stand tall for all that I believe in.
You can always count on me.

But sometimes I like to spice things up.

Or go a little nutty.

I have lots of friends:
Frosting,
Icing,
and my best friend...Ice Cream!

Ice Cream is so cool. He's the perfect sidekick for me.

And he can lick everyone at dodgeball. Ask anyone.

Ice Cream and I have been friends forever.
We love having fun and going to parties.
And we are always celebrating something.

Seems like it's someone's birthday every day!

But Ice Cream can also be bossy and loud at times.
When he wants something, he wants it right now!!
And that's really annoying to everyone.

He knocked over Hot Fudge to get first in line to go
out to recess. That made Hot Fudge even hotter!

Riding bikes, he shouted at Caramel,
"You move slower than molasses!"
That made things between them pretty sticky.

And when he demanded Sprinkles
but not Nuts come to a party, that
really whipped up Whipped Cream!

I tried to tell my friend to chill out, that no one would want to play with him if he was mean and always wanting his way.

But he didn't listen to me.
Instead he had a giant meltdown and screamed at me,
"You're so dense! What do you know?"

That took the cake.

It was not fun for anyone to get screamed at.
It hurt so much we all got a brain freeze.

That's when Gelato said, "Arrivederci"
and Sorbet added, "Au revoir."

Even Candle got burned out and left in a huff,
and Ice Cream realized he was all alone.

Ice Cream felt very lonely and very sad.

But then, Ice Cream realized something important.
One is not a party.

And friends bring out the best in each other…if you let them.

That's when, lickety-split,
Ice Cream made a complete swirl.

From then on his actions took on a very different flavor.
He apologized to everyone and gave me a giant hug.

That brought the two of us side by side again.
Ice Cream was even melting a bit.
He became his sweet, soft self again.

And that was the true icing on this Cake.

Note to Parents, Caregivers, and Educators

Cake & I Scream! is a story of Cake and his best friend, Ice Cream. Ice Cream tries to get his way by being bossy and loud. When this results in Ice Cream feeling all alone, Ice Cream has an important realization that changes his bossy ways. Working through this conflict reaffirms the friendship between Cake and Ice Cream and shows that being bossy isn't sweet at all.

What Is Bossiness?

While it is normal for kids to exert their independence and will, that does not mean it's okay to do so in ways that upset others. Bossiness is ordering others about in a domineering and oppressive manner. Bossy behaviors in children include: telling other kids what to do (e.g., where to sit, who to play with at recess), and what they are doing wrong; interrupting all the time; always needing to win at games; and having trouble waiting for their turn.

There are many reasons children exhibit bossy behavior, including but not limited to: seeking attention when not feeling heard or respected, testing the limits of their authority, having worries or frustrations that their own needs will not be met, expressing an insecurity or low self-esteem, wanting to express power and control (as someone who feels they have none), and wanting to express independence but in an immature manner.

Assertiveness, as opposed to bossiness, is being confident and forceful while still being mindful and sensitive of others. Similarly, being a leader is not about being controlling of others. Non-bossy assertive or leadership behavior is supportive, helps others find their strengths, encourages problem solving, promotes respect, and is considerate of the feelings of others.

While there are gender differences in how we perceive the same behavior (i.e., girls can be accused of being bossy while boys are seen as leaders), bossy behavior in the context of friendships will surely be experienced by any child as very unpleasant regardless of gender.

If Your Child Is Exhibiting Bossy Behaviors

The following are some ways to address bossy behaviors. Remember it takes some time to change one's ways. Be patient with your child as they navigate to appropriately assertive behavior. As always, change requires a lot of repetition.

- **Model respect.** Try making a practice of saying "please," "thank you," and "excuse me" all the time with one another at home. Pay attention to how you ask your kids to help out. Does it sound more like, "Clear the dishes off the table!" or "Can you please help me clear the table, honey, so we can get the kitchen cleaned up?" Use a proper apology as needed, such as, "I'm sorry, honey, but I was distracted by your little brother and I didn't realize you needed help with your shoes." Take the time to offer explanations (e.g., telling your child why something cannot happen right now) as a way of showing respect to your child through good communication. Your child is likely to echo your calm, respectful, and positive delivery when talking to peers and friends.

- **Offer up small ways your child can be in charge.** Give your child the ability to make choices for themselves when possible. For example, you could give your child a choice of which of two or three outfits to wear, whether you should have green or yellow vegetables for dinner, or whether they would like to help with raking the leaves or emptying the trash. This gives them a sense of control over some aspects of their lives. Remember, this is about offering your child choices, not overly negotiating with your child.

- **Be engaged.** When your child feels consistently heard and attended to they will likely feel more secure and confident. Play games together as a family where everyone is actually paying attention to each other and the game (without distractions—so please turn off electronics!). This can also help everyone be mindful of the experience of having fun with a game, rather than being focused on winning. And reward positive behavior by saying something like, "You did such a nice job playing with your brother, taking turns, and listening to him!"

- **Role-play.** Through role-play a child may learn to recognize what bossiness sounds like, and feel for the first time what it's like to be on the receiving end of bossy behavior. Pretend to be different characters, one of which bosses the other around. Have your child take turns playing both roles. In this role-play there are "do-overs" in which the same scene now is changed and the characters figure out how to conduct themselves in a nicer way.

- **Set expectations.** Before a playdate, talk to your child about expectations including treating others nicely and fairly (e.g., taking turns, and letting others choose what activities they want to do). Remind your child that other children have feelings that can get hurt when they are mistreated and that friends will pull away if they are bossed around and will probably form other friendships with kids who act more pleasantly.

- **Be creative.** Play creative games where bossy behavior is channeled into appropriate expressions of assertiveness. For example, imagine your child is the teacher and you are a student in their classroom. Or they are the doctor and you are a patient who has come for an appointment after not feeling well. Help your child see what someone in charge such as a teacher or doctor can sound like when they are expressing themselves in nice ways.

- **Support the team approach.** Team sports are a great way to dilute bossy behavior and try to turn it into more appropriate leadership skills. Since team sports encourage kids to work together, there is less room for individual children to take control; rather, figuring out how to come together and work as a unit is the name of the game. At the same time, some children will emerge as leaders of a team, but with guidance, they can do so without hurting others.

If Your Child Is on the Receiving End of Bossy Behavior

If your child is the one being bossed about by a friend, first explore with your child what exactly is happening in order to clarify the circumstances. Then, talk to your child about what they are feeling and discuss how best to handle these situations, taking into account your child's manner and disposition. The following are some ideas to help. If you suspect your child is being bullied (which is different from being bossed around), seek help from your child's teacher, principal, or a mental healthcare professional.

- **More role-play.** If your child is being bossed around by a friend, it's important they learn how to confidently stand up for themselves. Teach your child what this sounds like, particularly if you sense your child is hesitant to do so. Role-play can be a useful way of demonstrating how to stand up to a friend assertively and clearly. Try out different replies your child can use, such as, "No, thanks, I'd rather decide for myself," "I don't like it when you talk to me that way," "It's rude when you tell me what to do," or "I can make my own choices. Really." You might even try humor, such as "Aye aye, Captain!" or "Yes, sir boss-man, sir!" as long as it's clear this is making fun of the bossiness and an attempt to deflate it.

- **Offer alternatives.** Create opportunities for your child to play with different children so they can experience children who do not boss them around.

They can then make their own choices about how they want to spend their friendship time. Your child will be less likely to accept bossy behavior after noticing the difference with friends who are nicer.

- **Remind your child they can walk away.** Teach your child that they have a choice in defining their friendships and that they can get up and walk away when a friend will not stop behaving badly. If your child wants to continue to play with the friend who has bossy tendencies, they can actually help shape the friendship in a positive way by only spending time with this friend when the friend is behaving well, and putting distance between them when the friend is not. Your child must be prepared that their friend may not take the feedback well and may become defensive (for example, saying something like "you're just being a baby!"). If this continues, discuss with your child if this is really a positive friendship and one that is worth preserving if the other friend is not able to listen and modify their behavior.

- **Evaluate friendships.** Talk to your child about using their feelings to help evaluate friendships.

Let your child know that friendships should make them feel good about themselves and ought to be fun and supportive. If a friend is using a kind of threat or emotional pressure such as, "I will not be your friend if you don't do as I say" and this makes your child feel anxious and upset, these feelings are actually a helpful guide, telling your child there is something not right about what this friend said. Remind your child that they are in control of themselves unless they give this control away to someone else.

Helping children socialize in friendly, cooperative ways has a profoundly positive impact for life. As children learn how to develop appropriately assertive behavior they will also increase their self-confidence. With adult guidance, learning these skills is very possible. If your child continues to struggle with bossy or passive behavior in friendships, it could also be time to seek professional help from a clinical psychologist or other licensed mental health professional who can help assess the situation and offer additional interventions.

About the Author

Michael Genhart, PhD, is a licensed clinical psychologist in private practice in San Francisco and Mill Valley, California. He lives with his family in Marin County. He received his BA in psychology from the University of California, San Diego and his PhD in clinical and community psychology from the University of Maryland, College Park. He is the author of several picture books including: *Ouch! Moments: When Words Are Used in Hurtful Ways* (2016), *So Many Smarts!* (2017), *Peanut Butter & Jellyous* (2017), *Mac & Geeeez!* (2017), and *I See You* (2017), all from Magination Press, as well as *Yes We Are!* (Little Pickle Press, 2018).

About the Illustrator

Steve Mack grew up a prairie boy on Canada's Great Plains and has drawn for as long as he can remember. His first lessons in art were taught to him by watching his grandfather do paint-by-numbers at the summer cottage. He has worked for greeting card companies and has illustrated several books. Steve lives in a beautiful valley in a turn-of-the-century farmhouse with his wife and two children.

About Magination Press

Magination Press is an imprint of the American Psychological Association, the largest scientific and professional organization representing psychologists in the United States and the largest association of psychologists worldwide.